A Cat Called Max

Magnificent Max

Barron's Arch Book Series

A Cat Called Max

Magnificent Max

Terrance Dicks

Illustrated by Toni Goffe

New York • Toronto

First edition for the United States, Canada and the Philippines
published 1990 by Barron's Educational Series, Inc.

First published 1989 by Piccadilly Press Ltd., London, England

All inquiries should be addressed to:
Barron's Educational Series, Inc.
250 Wireless Boulevard
Hauppauge, New York 11788

International Standard Book No. 0-8120-4427-4

Library of Congress Catalog Card No. 89-38134

Library of Congress Cataloging-in-Publication Data

Dicks, Terrance.
    Magnificent Max / Terrance Dicks; illustrated by Toni Goffe. —
1st ed. for the U.S., Canada, and the Philippines.
        p.   cm. — (A Cat called Max) (Barron's arch book series)
    "First published 1989 by Piccadilly Press Ltd., London,
England" —Verso t.p.
    Summary: A sophisticated talking cat named Max appears in
the aftermath of a huge storm, befriends a family, and has
adventures with its members.
    ISBN 0-8120-4427-4
    [1. Cats—Fiction.]   I. Goffe, Toni, ill.   II. Title.
III. Series.   IV. Series: Dicks, Terrance. Cat called Max.
PZ7.D5627Mag   1990
[Fic]—dc20   89-38134
                                                        CIP
                                                        AC

PRINTED IN THE UNITED STATES OF AMERICA
0123 3900 987654321

Contents

Chapter One

Enter Max

Max arrived on the night of the great storm.

It was the worst storm that anyone could remember for years and years.

Rain lashed down in torrents, thunder growled, lightning flashed and great gusts of wind rattled the windows. Timmy lay in bed, in his little attic bedroom, listening to the howling of the storm. He wondered if the roof would blow off.

Several times his mom and dad came in to ask if he was all right. Timmy said he was fine. To be honest he was rather enjoying it all.

Suddenly there came an enormous crashing explosion and a blinding flash, so bright that Timmy could see it clear through the bedroom curtains. The whole house seemed to shake.

This time Timmy really was scared, and he jumped out of bed and ran downstairs.

He found his parents in the kitchen, staring out of the window at brightly flickering flames. The big old oak tree in the backyard was on fire! "Must have been a thunderbolt," said Timmy's dad. "I'd better go and check. We don't want the fire to spread."

Timmy begged to be allowed to come as well, and after a certain amount of fuss his father said he could.

Timmy put on his big waterproof raincoat over his pajamas and pulled on his boots and his rainhat. Then he followed his dad out into the howling storm.

He would never have believed that going out into your own backyard could be such an adventure.

The bushes close to the house were lashing to and fro, like monsters reaching out to grab you, and the oak tree was blazing like a roman candle, hissing and sputtering in the wind-driven rain.

Luckily the tree was well away from the house and the backyard fence so there didn't seem to be much danger of the fire spreading.

Timmy and his father stood looking in fascination at the blazing tree. Suddenly there came a roaring, clattering sound from overhead, so loud it even rose above the howling of the storm. They looked up and saw a light in the sky. A lightning flash revealed a gleaming metal shape, flying quite low overhead.

"It's a helicopter," said Timmy's father. "One of those big army ones.

I wonder what brings them out on a
night like this."

As Timmy stepped back to get a
better look, he stumbled over
something wet and soft and soggy on
the ground. There was an indignant
yowl.

He looked down and saw a black furry shape at his feet. He knelt down to examine it. "It's a cat, a big black cat. I think it must be hurt."

Timmy's father bent down to have a look. "Maybe it was in the tree when the lightning struck. Lucky to be alive, poor thing."

Timmy said, "It's alive all right, judging by that yowl. Maybe it was only stunned. Anyway, we'd better take care of it."

Carefully he lifted up the cat, which was surprisingly big and heavy, and carried it into the house.

Chapter Two

Max Makes Himself at Home

Staggering under the weight of the big cat, Timmy carried it back up the garden path and into the brightly-lit warm kitchen.

His mother was making hot chocolate. "What on earth have you got there?"

While Timmy's dad explained about finding the cat in the backyard, Timmy settled the bedraggled creature on the mat. He got his mother to give him an old towel and began rubbing gently at the wet tangled fur.

It was a big, handsome creature with a long aristocratic face, rather like the cats you see on Egyptian temples. In the light, Timmy could see it wasn't completely black after all. Under its chin was a sort of white bib, making the big cat look as if it were wearing evening dress.

"He certainly is a whopper," said Timmy's father. "Biggest cat I've ever seen!"

His mother poured some of the hot chocolate milk into a saucer. "See if you can get it to drink some of this warm milk."

The cat opened an astonishingly large slanting green eye and said distinctly, "I'd much prefer a large brandy, dear lady—if it's not

putting you to too much trouble, that is?"

Timmy's father was so astonished that he just said politely, "I beg your pardon?"

"Brandy," said the cat impatiently. When a fellow's been practically shipwrecked, he needs something stronger than milk."

"How about some warm milk with brandy in it?" suggested Timmy, doing his best to be tactful.

The cat yawned and stretched. "Yesss. . ." it hissed softly. "Brandy and hot milk, the very thing. What an intelligent child!"

Timmy's father went to the kitchen cupboard and got the bottle of brandy that he kept for "medicinal purposes." His mother poured some milk into a saucer.

The cat gave her a pained look. "In a cup, dear lady, if you don't mind, in a cup."

Timmy's mother, who, like his father, was still looking pretty dazed, poured some milk into a mug.

His father added a hefty slug of brandy.

The cat uncoiled itself from the mat and sank down into the old kitchen armchair, crossing its legs.

Reaching out a long arm it took

the cup and drained it in a single swig,
shuddering with pleasure. "Ah that's
better . . . . By the way, my name is
Maximillian. No need to stand on
ceremony, though—you can call me
Max."

It looked at them expectantly.

Timmy was the first to recover. "How
do you do, er, Max?" he said politely.
"My name is Timothy. This is my
mother, Mrs. Tompkins, and this is my
father, Mr. Tompkins."

"Charmed, I'm sure," said Max graciously. He held out a paw, and Mr. and Mrs. Tompkins shook it in turn.

It was rather like being received by royalty, and Mrs. Tompkins said later she had a distinct impulse to curtsey.

"I've got an older brother, Jim, but he's away," Timmy went on. "And a younger sister, Samantha, but she's asleep."

"Though how she can sleep through all this," said Timmy's mother. The storm was still howling around the house, though it seemed to be dying down just a little.

Max yawned and stretched. "I'm pretty tired myself to tell you the truth. Now then, where am I going to sleep?"

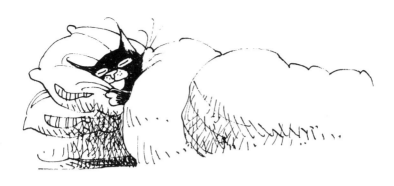

Chapter Three

Life with Max

The Tompkins family all looked at each other.

"Er, you'll be staying then?" asked Mr. Tompkins faintly.

"Very decent of you," said Max. "Well, if you insist. Just till things get sorted out. Now then, where are you going to put me?"

The Tompkins family looked at one another.

"You can sleep on my bed," said Timmy.

"Too kind," drawled Max. "But what about you?"

"I said on, not in," said Timmy. "I'll be in the bed, you can sleep at the bottom. There's plenty of room for us both."

The next morning, Timmy woke up feeling that his bed had suddenly become very hard.

When he opened his eyes, Timmy understood why.

He was curled up on the bedroom rug with a blanket over him. Max was comfortably stretched out in bed, cradled in the soft pillows.

Timmy jumped up with a yell. "Max!"

Max opened one eye. "Please don't shout . . . . Now that's much better. It's far too early for noise."

"What am I doing on the floor?"

Max opened his other eye. "Must have rolled off during the night, dear boy. Slept like a top myself."

Timmy gave him a suspicious look, then struggled into his warm bathrobe. He went to look out of the window and gave a gasp of amazement.

Normally his window looked out on a row of peaceful suburban gardens.

Now it was a scene of amazing chaos and confusion.

His father's prize flower beds had been practically shredded, and the charred stump of the blasted oak tree loomed over their ruined garden. "Come and look at this!"

Max uncoiled himself from the bed and strolled over to the window.

"Yesss," he drawled. "Blew up quite

a storm last night by the looks of it." He
sniffed. "Do I smell coffee?"

They went downstairs and found
Timmy's mother cooking breakfast in the
kitchen.

His sister Samantha was in her high
chair eating cornflakes—or rather
spreading them all around the place as
usual.

"Pussy cat!" she yelled when she saw
Max. "Here, puss!"

Max looked thoughtfully at her.
"Yesss . . . ." He slid into a chair.
"Now then, what's for breakfast?"

Timmy's mom glanced under the
table, where Nibs, the family cat,
was gobbling up half a can of cat food.
"I don't suppose you'd care for
some—no, you probably wouldn't."

(It was interesting, thought Timmy,
that Nibs completely ignored Max,
treating him not as another cat
but another person.)

"Ah, the perfect breakfast," said
Max. "Bacon, eggs, toast and
jam and coffee. Nothing like
it!"

Timmy's mother gave him a look.
"Well, since it's Sunday . . . . We
usually try to have a good hearty
breakfast on the weekends. Things are a
little different Monday to Friday."

"I'm sure I shall manage very well," murmured Max obligingly.

Samantha yelled, "Milk for pussy!" and threw the remains of her bowl of cornflakes and milk all over him. Just for a moment, Max's green eyes flared angrily and Timmy froze, feeling something dreadful was going to happen. "No, Max," he yelled.

The green flare died down and Max said, "Thank you, my dear, most delicious!" An astonishingly long tongue shot out and licked the milk from his face and whiskers.

Samantha chuckled with delight.

Timmy got the orange juice carton from the refrigerator and poured some for himself and Max. "Shouldn't we let someone know we've found you?" he asked.

Suddenly the angry look was back on Max's face. "Let who know?"

"Well, somebody must be looking for you . . . ." Timmy broke off, distracted by the drone of a helicopter somewhere overhead. "They've probably reported you missing. Should we tell the police, for instance?"

"Tell nobody," snapped Max. Then he managed a smile. "No need to trouble your wonderful policemen about me."

Timmy's father came in, his face filled with gloom and despair.

"What's the matter, Dad?"

"What's the matter! Have you looked outside?"

Timmy thought his father must be mourning his lost flowers. "It's a pity about the flower beds, Dad, but we'll soon get them looking nice again. Don't know what we can do about the tree, though."

"I'm not talking about the back," yelled his father. "Have you seen the state of things in the front? Half the trees in the street have blown over— and one of them's landed smack on top of our car!"

Chapter Four

Max's Magic

Timmy followed his father out into the street, and Max strolled after them. The scene in the street was even more amazing than it was out the back.

As Timmy's dad had said, several of the trees in the street had been blown right over.

But the tree that Timmy's father was worried about was the old sycamore right in front of the house.

It had toppled over sideways and was now resting right on top of their car, pinning it to the ground.

"We'll have to get a crane or something, and that'll take ages. Judging by the news, there's damage like this all over the place," said Timmy's father gloomily.

A voice behind them drawled, "Bit of a problem, eh? Can I help?" Max had followed them out of the house and was looking at the scene with an air of mild amusement.

A helicopter roared overhead, and Timmy looked up. "Help? I really don't see how . . . ." He looked back at Max, and was just in time to see a black and white streak disappearing inside the house.

The helicopter droned away, and seconds later Max reappeared. "Do

forgive me. That beastly machine
startled me. Never could stand loud
noises. Now then, where were we? Oh
yes, a bit of a problem with the old
car." Before anyone could say anything
he sprang onto the trunk of the fallen
tree and began lashing his tail.

Suddenly the fallen tree trunk started to shudder. Then, as Max sprang clear, it rolled neatly from the top of the car and into the road.

Timmy and his father stood gaping in amazement.

Timmy's father moved forward, peering at the car. "It's made a nasty dent in the top I'm afraid . . . ."

He jumped back as something black and glossy flashed past him. It was Max, taking a flying leap onto the top of the battered car. For a moment he just stood there, his four legs spread wide. Then he began to purr, a deep vibrating sound that was almost a roar.

The car began to shudder, just like the tree . . . .

Then with a loud "Spang!" the dent undented itself.

Max jumped down from the roof.
"There you go! Now, how about a bit of
breakfast?"

They all went back into the kitchen
and soon Max was happily digging into
bacon and eggs.

He waved aside their attempts to
thank him. "Just a knack, you know,
nothing to it really." Once he'd
cleaned his plate, Max rose to his feet,
bowed to Timmy's mother and kissed
her hand.

"Delicious, dear lady, absolutely delicious. Now, if you'll excuse me? I usually take a little catnap about this time. Something light at about one o'clock perhaps? Fish, a little dry white wine, a green salad . . . nothing elaborate." With a lordly wave of farewell, Max strolled from the room.

For a moment the family just looked at each other in stunned silence. The silence was broken by the distant sound of deep, rattling snores, drifting down from Timmy's room at the top of the house.

"Well!" exploded Timmy's mother. "If that cat thinks this is the Ritz Hotel, he can think again! Fish with a little dry white wine indeed."

"Oh, it's only his way," said Timmy. "He can have fishsticks and a Coke like the rest of us."

"He was really helpful about the car," said Timmy's father, and told Timmy's mother all about what had happened. "It was all pretty impressive, I can tell you. Max certainly isn't just any old cat."

"Well, his manners are very nice," she said. "Quite distinguished, really. But he does take rather a lot for granted, doesn't he? I mean, where does he come from—and how long is he staying?"

"I suppose I ought to ask him," said Mr. Tompkins. "Only, I don't like to somehow. There's something very unusual about Max, you know."

"Like talking, you mean?" suggested Timmy. "Not to mention walking on his hind legs when he wants to, and eating with a knife and fork and moving tree trunks by mystic mind-power?"

"Yes, there's all that," agreed Timmy's father.

But that wasn't really what he'd been talking about, as Timmy knew very well.

The walking and talking and everything would have been totally amazing in any ordinary cat, but with Max you just accepted it all. Max had such a magnificent air about him that all his powers seemed quite

28

natural, and his lightest wish felt like a royal command.

"Oh, yes," said Timmy. "There's something special about Max all right."

And something very mysterious as well, he thought.

But he still didn't know just how special and mysterious Max really was . . . .

Chapter Five

Speedway Max

Timmy and his father spent the rest of the morning clearing up the backyard. There wasn't really that much damage. Apart from the lightning-blasted oak tree they'd gotten off pretty lightly.

Timmy's mom called them in for lunch, and Max came down and ate his fishsticks and Coke perfectly happily. He sipped his Coke thoughtfully and said, "Unassuming little local wine, eh? Interesting bouquet. And these long, narrow fish are delicious!"

On Sunday afternoons, they went for what Timmy's parents called "a nice little ride in the car."

To be honest, Timmy hated these "little rides" and usually pleaded to be left behind. The family car was old and slow, and his little sister Samantha usually got bored and acted up.

Timmy tried his best to get out of it again this time. "Maybe I'd better just stay home with Max. He won't want to come."

Unfortunately, Max didn't take the hint. "Little trip in the old jalopy? Nothing I'd like better, old chap."

As soon as they'd cleaned up after lunch, they all set off. Timmy's parents

were in the front of course, and he
was sitting in the back as usual
with Samantha, though this time
Max was perched on the seat
between them.

To get out into the country you had
to go along a short stretch of
speedway. It was the one part of the
trip that Timmy really dreaded.
His father was a rather timid and
cautious driver, and they always
moved along in the slow lane, other
cars zipping past them.

Quite a few of the drivers shouted out
rude comments, like, "Get that wreck
off the speedway!" as they whizzed
past.

Sure enough, they were picked on
again.

It was a big, red sports car this time,
driven by some creep with an

open-necked shirt revealing a hairy chest
complete with a dangling gold
medallion.

   With a blare of its multi-toned horn
it swept past them, cutting in
dangerously close and making
Timmy's father wobble dangerously.
He gave a feeble toot of protest on his
little horn, and as the sports car drew
away, its driver waved his fist at them in
a very rude way.

"The fellow's a road hog," said Max indignantly from the back seat. "Why don't you teach him a lesson?"

"In this car?" said Timmy's father hopelessly. "Besides, I'm not exactly Mario Andretti, you know."

"Just you leave that to me," said Max.

Max started to purr. Suddenly the whole car seemed to be humming with energy. Timmy's father said later that it was like finding yourself at the wheel of the biggest, newest, most powerful car you could imagine.

It also felt, he said, as if the car were driving itself.

With a roar of power that somehow mingled with Max's purr, the old family heap streaked ahead, leaving the creep in the flashy red sports car behind—almost as if he were standing still.

As they zoomed past, Timmy turned and gave the sports car driver a little wave out of the back window.

For just a second he saw the other driver's face, purple with rage, then sports car and driver were a fast-dwindling dot far behind them.

Timmy's father couldn't help feeling a glow of pride as the car sped smoothly along the speedway.

But the glow faded at the sight of a flashing light ahead. "Oh, no," gasped Timmy. "It's the cops!"

Timmy's father drew in behind
the police car and switched off the
engine. "Afternoon, officer," he said
nervously. "Anything wrong?" The
policeman was very large and he
looked very stern in his cap and
dark glasses. "You have just passed
a radar check, sir. Are you aware
that you were traveling at precisely
79.9 miles per hour?"

Timmy's father gulped.

"It's not just that you were doing
nearly eighty," said the policeman,
taking off his dark glasses and

speaking in a more normal voice. "It's the fact that you were doing it in an old rattletrap like this. What have you got under that hood, a jet engine?"

"Just your normal family sedan, officer," said Timmy's father with a nervous laugh. "Mind you, I take pride in keeping it well maintained."

The policeman gave him a skeptical look. "If I could see your driver's license, sir?"

Timmy's father handed it over and the policeman checked it and handed it back. "Now then," he began. "What about this speeding?"

Before Timmy's father could reply, they heard a roaring sound and a red blur came flashing towards them. It was the creep in the sports car, determined to avenge his humiliation. As he shot past he

turned and delivered a V-sign—
straight in the face of the amazed
policeman.

"Hey, you!" said the policeman
furiously. He turned and ran back to his
police car and jumped in. With a
screeching of tires, the police car roared
off in pursuit of the unfortunate road
hog.

Timmy couldn't help grinning.
"That'll teach him!"

His father drew a deep breath. "Look, if nobody minds, I think we'll abandon this trip and go home. I've had just about all the excitement I can stand for one day."

They drove on until they found an exit, and headed for home. But when they reached their street they couldn't get into it. The street was blocked and a policeman was standing by the barrier.

"What the devil is going on?" said Timmy's father, stopping the car.

By now Timmy had a pretty good idea—and his suspicions were confirmed when Max leaned past him and opened the car door. "Where do you think you're off to, Max?"

"Oh, I thought I'd be on my way. I really can't impose on you any more."

Timmy slammed the car door shut. "I don't know what kind of trouble you're in Max—but you'll stand a better chance with us helping you than on your own."

Max still looked worried. But he sat there quietly as the policeman came up to the car. "I'm afraid this road is closed, sir."

"But we live here," protested Timmy's mother. "At number eleven!"

The policeman checked his list.

"The Tompkins family, is it? You're the ones we've been waiting for," he said. "Everyone else has been checked." The policeman waved them on. They drove up to their house—and found a huge army tank parked outside!

Something told Timmy that Max was in big trouble.

Chapter Six

Max in Trouble

There were army trucks too, as well as the tank, and the whole street was closed. Timmy's father parked beside the tank and they all got out of the car. Immediately they were surrounded by armed soldiers.

"Mr. Tompkins and family?" asked the sergeant in charge.

"That's right. What's going on?"

"Just go on into the house, sir."

They all went into the house and

into the living room—all except Max who slipped past everyone else and disappeared upstairs.

Three men were waiting in the living room. One wore the uniform of a General. The second wore an old tweed suit. He had big, thick glasses and a high-domed bald head. The third man was handsome and elegant in an expensive-looking pinstriped suit.

They introduced themselves, and although Timmy didn't quite catch their names he realized that, as well as a General, their visitors were a Very Important Scientist and a Man from the State Department.

"I must apologize for disturbing you like this, Mr. Tompkins," said the Man from the State Department smoothly, "and, indeed, for entering your house without permission."

"I should think so, too," said Timmy's father. "Nerve, I call it. What do you mean by it?"

"This is a National Emergency," barked the General, adding mysteriously, "we have Special Powers."

After that it was the Scientist who did most of the talking. "I'm sure you remember last night's freak storm. Now, did anything . . . unusual happen that night?"

"I should say it did," said Timmy's father. "Our oak tree caught fire, for a start, and all my flower beds were ruined."

"Anything else?" asked the Scientist impatiently. "Anything else really strange?"

"Why do you ask?" said Timmy. "I think you ought to tell us what's going on."

The Scientist looked at the General, who nodded briefly.

"Now, all this is very confidential," said the Scientist. "But for some time we've been monitoring a fresh crop of UFO sightings—a UFO, as I'm sure you know, is an Unidentified Flying Object."

"You mean a flying saucer?" asked Timmy's mother. "I should think you'd have better things to do with your time."

"This particular UFO is real enough, believe me," said the Scientist. "We think Earth is being observed by creatures from another planet, perhaps even from another dimension."

"What's all this got to do with us?" asked Timmy's mother.

"Last night we got the most positive sighting ever. We tracked the UFO as best we could on radar, but of course everything was thrown off by the freak storm."

"We regarded the matter as so urgent that we had helicopters searching, even in the storm," said the General, "but the weather threw them off course and they lost sight of the UFO."

"Suddenly the object disappeared from all our tracking screens," the Scientist went on. "And as far as we can work out, the UFO vanished somewhere very close to where we are now!"

"So what we want to know is this," said the General sternly. "Did you see any strange alien creature on the night of the storm?"

"What would this alien look like?" asked Timmy.

"It could look like anything," said the Scientist. "We believe they've been monitoring our broadcasts, so it could even speak our language."

"What will happen to the alien if you find it?" asked Timmy. No one seemed to mind that he was doing all the talking.

"It will have to be quarantined," said the Scientist immediately. "Locked up in a sterile high-security environment. Then it will have to be subjected to tests and experiments. We must learn as much about it as we can."

"It will have to be interrogated as well," growled the General. "We must learn its motive for spying on us," said the Man from the State Department. "Maybe its people plan to invade Earth."

"Maybe it was just curious?" said Timmy, but no one listened.

"Well," said the General sternly. "Have you anything to tell us? I warn you, there will be severe consequences if you hold anything back."

Timmy's mother and father looked uncertainly at each other, and then at Timmy.

Suddenly Timmy knew what he had to do. "As a matter of fact a strange alien creature did arrive on the night of the storm. We took him in and we've been looking after him. Wait here and I'll get him." Timmy ran upstairs. Minutes later he returned, carrying Max in his arms. "Here he is. We found him half-drowned in the garden."

He put Max down and the cat ran around the room on all fours, rubbing at the General's ankles and looking up at him.

The General bent down and rubbed the cat's chin. Max purred contentedly. "Well, you're a fine fellow, aren't you. But you're not what we're looking for." He looked at the others and laughed. "Not unless the Earth is about to be invaded by pussy cats from outer space, right?"

Pretty soon after this the visitors left, convinced they must look elsewhere for their alien monster.

Timmy and his parents saw them off. They returned to the living room to find Max stretched out in an armchair, mopping his brow. "That was a close one." He looked at Timmy's father. "You couldn't spare a spot of more brandy and milk? Just for medicinal purposes, you know."

That night Timmy snuggled down under the covers with Max purring gently at the end of his bed.

"Thanks for the help, old chap," said Max. "Jolly decent of you to risk getting in trouble for me."

"That's all right," said Timmy. "Glad you had the sense to play along. Anyway, I told them the truth, didn't I? Not my fault if they didn't believe me!"

"I didn't mean any harm, you know," said Max. "Just curious, like you said, and got a bit too close."

"That's what I thought."

"So I can stay with you for a bit, take a look around?"

Timmy thought over all the amazing and magical events of the day. "Certainly, Max, my dear fellow," he said sleepily. "You can stay just as long as you like!"

Other *Arch Books* that you will enjoy reading

About the Author

After studying at Cambridge, Terrance Dicks became an advertising copy-writer, then a radio and television scriptwriter and script editor. His career as an author began with the *Dr. Who* series and he has now written a variety of other books on subjects ranging from horror to detection. Barron's publishes several of his series, including *The Adventures of Goliath* and *T. R. Bear*.

About the Illustrator

Toni Goffe is married and has two sons. He has written and illustrated many children's books, including *Ms. Wiz Spells Trouble* in the Arch Book Series.

More Exciting Adventures With Arch Books

Arch Books are Barron's gripping mini-novels for children of various reading ages. Each of the titles in this series offers the young reader a special adventure. The stories are packed with action, humor, mystery, chilling thrills and even a bit of magic! Each paperback book boasts 12 to 24 handsome line-art illustrations. Each book: $2.95, Can. $3.95

Arch Book Titles:

BEN AND THE CHILD OF THE FOREST
Mira Lobe, Illustrated by Franz S. Sklenitzka
ISBN: 0-8120-3936-X (Ages 7-9)

THE BLUEBEARDS: Adventure on Skull Island
Tony Bradman, Illustrated by Rowan Barnes Murphy
ISBN: 0-8120-4421-5 (Ages 8-11)

THE BLUEBEARDS: Mystery at Musket Bay
Tony Bradman, Illustrated by Rowan Barnes Murphy
ISBN: 0-8120-4422-3 (Ages 8-11)

CAROLINE MOVES IN
Lene Mayer-Skumanz, Illustrated by Franz S. Sklenitzka
ISBN: 0-8120-3938-6 (Ages 6-8)

A CAT CALLED MAX: Magnificent Max
Terrance Dicks, Illustrated by Toni Goffe
ISBN: 0-8120-4427-4 (Ages 8-11)

INTO THE NIGHT HOUSE
Heather Eyles, Illustrated by Adriano Gon
ISBN: 0-8120-4423-1 (Ages 9-12)

MS WIZ SPELLS TROUBLE
Terence Blacker, Illustrated by Toni Goffe
ISBN: 0-8120-4420-7 (Ages 8-11)

THE RED SPORTS CAR
Franz S. Sklenitzka, Illustrated by the author
ISBN: 0-8120-3937-8 (Ages 6-8)

All prices are in U.S. and Canadian dollars and subject to change without notice. At your bookstore, or order direct adding 10% postage (minimum charge $1.50). N.Y. residents add sales tax.

Barron's Educational Series, Inc.
250 Wireless Blvd., Hauppauge, NY 11788
Call toll-free: 1-800-645-3476 In NY 1-800-257-5729
In Canada: Georgetown Book Warehouse, 34 Armstrong Ave.,
Georgetown, Ont. L7G 4R9
Call toll-free: 1-800-668-4336